M'HASHISH

by

Mohammed Mrabet

Taped and translated from

the Moghrebi by

PAUL BOWLES

City Lights Books
San Francisco

ISBN: 0-87286-034-5
LC Card Number: 70-88228

Cover design by Rex Ray

Front cover painting by Mohammed Mrabet

Portrait of Mrabet is from a photograph
        by Terrence Spencer
Title page art by Gent Sturgeon

Visit our website: www.citylights.com

CITY LIGHTS BOOKS are edited by Lawrence Ferlinghetti
and Nancy J. Peters and published at the City Lights Bookstore,
261 Columbus Avenue, San Francisco, CA 94133.

M'HASHISH

Mohammed
Mrabet

M'HASHISH

THE CANEBRAKE

Kacem and Stito met every afternoon at a café. They were old friends. Kacem drank, and he had a wife whom he never allowed to go out of the house. No matter how much she entreated him and argued with him, he would not even let her go to the hammam to bathe. Stito had no troubles because he was a bachelor, and only smoked kif.

Kacem would come into the café with a bottle in his shopping bag, and soon both of them would go on to Kacem's house. On the way they would stop at the market to buy food, since Kacem would not permit his wife to go to market, either. Stito had no one to cook for him, and so he ate each night at Kacem's house, and always paid his share.

They would carry the food to Kacem's wife so she could prepare it. First, however, she would make tapas for Kacem's drinks, and tea for Stito's kif. Later when the food was cooking she would go in and sit with the two men.

Once when they were all sitting there together, Stito turned to Kacem and said: Sometimes I wonder how you can drink so much. Where do you store it all?

Kacem laughed. And you? You don't get

anything but smoke out of your pipe. I get the alcohol right inside me, and it feels wonderful.

That's an empty idea you have, said Stito. Kif gives me more pleasure than alcohol could ever give anybody. And it makes me think straighter and talk better.

Kacem's wife decided that this was a good moment to say to her husband: Your friend's right. You drink too much.

Kacem was annoyed. Go and look at the food, he told her. It ought to be ready. We want to eat.

She brought the dinner in, and they set to work eating it. After they had finished, they talked for a half hour or so, and then Stito stood up. Until tomorrow, he told Kacem.

Yes, yes. Until tomorrow, said Kacem, who was drunk.

If Allah wills, Stito added.

Kacem's wife got up and opened the door for him.

Good night.

She shut the door, and then she and Kacem went to bed. Feeling full of love, she began to kiss her husband. But he only lay there, too drunk to notice her.

Soon she sat up and began to complain. From the day of our wedding you've never loved me, she said. You never pay me any attention at all unless you want to eat.

Go to sleep, woman, he told her.

She had started to cry, and it was a long time before she slept.

The next afternoon when he finished work, Kacem went to the café to meet Stito. They did the marketing and carried the food back to Kacem's house. The evening passed the same as always. Kacem was very drunk by the time Stito was ready to go home.

Kacem's wife opened the door for Stito and stepped outside. As he went through the doorway she whispered: Try and come alone tomorrow. Let him come by himself.

What do you mean? he said.

She pointed at the canebrake behind the garden. Hide there, she said.

Stito understood. But he'll be here, he whispered.

That's all right. Don't worry, she told him. Good night.

Good night.

The woman shut the door. Kacem was still sitting there drinking. She left him there and went to bed.

Again the following afternoon the two friends met in the café. Stito put away his pipe. How are you? he said.

Let's go, said Kacem. He was eager to get home and open his bottle.

I can't go right now, Stito told him. I've got to wait here and see somebody. I'll come later. Here's the money for the food.

Yes, said Kacem. I'll go on to the market, then.

Sit down with me a minute, said Stito.

No, no. I'll be going.

I'll see you later, Stito said.

Stito sat there in the café until dusk, and then he got up and went to the street where Kacem's house was. He waited until no one was passing by before he began to make his way through the canebrake. He was invisible in here. He peered between the canes and saw Kacem sitting in his room with a bottle on the table beside him, and a glass in his hand. And he saw the woman bring in the taifor.

Then she came outside carrying a large basin, and walked straight to the edge of the canebrake. She set the basin down and bent over it as if she were working. She was facing her husband and talking with him, and her garments reached to the ground in front of her. In the back, however, she was completely uncovered, and Stito saw everything he wanted to

4

see. While she pretended to be washing something in the basin, she pushed her bare haunches back against the canes, and he pressed forward and began to enjoy himself with her.

When you're ready, she whispered, pull it out and let me catch it all in my hand.

That's no way, he said. How can I do that?

The woman moved forward suddenly and made it slip out, so that Stito understood that if he were to have anything at all with her, he would have to do as she wanted.

You can do it again afterwards and finish inside, if you like, she whispered.

She backed against the canes again, and he started once more. When he was almost ready he warned her, and she reached back with her hand, and got what she wanted. Keeping her fist shut, she waited so he could do it again the way he enjoyed it. He finished and went out of the canebrake into the street. No one saw him.

The woman walked into the house. She stood by the chair where Kacem sat, looking down at him. Can't I go to the hammam tomorrow? she said.

Are you starting that all over again? cried Kacem. I've told you no a thousand times. No! You can't leave this house.

She reached out her hand, opened it, and let what she had been holding drip into the taifor beside Kacem's glass.

Kacem stared. He had been drunk a moment before, and now he was no longer drunk. He did not even ask her from whom she had got it, or how. He stood up, leaving the bottle and glass, and went to bed without his dinner.

In the morning when he went out to work, Kacem left the door of his house wide open. All day he thought about his wife. When he had finished work, he went to the café to meet Stito.

His face was sad as he sat down. Fill me a pipe, he said.

What? Stito cried.

Yes.

Stito gave him his pipe. What's happened? It's the first time you've ever asked for kif.

I'm through with drinking, Kacem told him. I'm going to start smoking kif.

But why?

Kacem did not reply, and Stito did not ask again.

That evening the two friends arrived at Kacem's house laughing and joking, with their heads full of kif. Kacem was in a fine humor all evening. After Stito had gone, he said to his wife: You went to the hammam?

Yes, she said. Thank you for leaving the door open. I thought you'd forgotten to shut it when you went out.

I'm not going to lock it any more, he told her.

She kissed him and they went to bed. It was the first time in many nights that Kacem was not too drunk to play games with his wife. They made one another very happy, and finally they fell into a perfect sleep.

THE KIF PATCH

Outside the village of Rehreh there was a Rifi who lived alone. He owned a large tract of land on which there were many trees, and he made his living by cutting the trees and burning them into charcoal which he carried to the city.

One day when he had just sold his charcoal in the market, a Djibli came up to him and asked him if he had any work for him to do. The Rifi said that if he did not mind living in the country, he could come and work for him until the beginning of summer. The Djibli agreed, and together they went out to Rehreh, to the Rifi's house.

There's a shack over there where you can sleep, said the Rifi. Then he showed the Djibli around his property.

Tomorrow morning, incha'Allah, we'll cut some trees and make charcoal, he said. And if we finish early enough, we can plant a little kif here in this field.

Ouakha, said the Djibli. They had dinner, and the Djibli went out to his shack to sleep. In the morning the Rifi got up and made coffee. Then he went out and woke the Djibli and told him to come and have breakfast.

After they had eaten they smoked a few pipes of kif together, and then they went out and began to chop down trees. They would work a while, sit down and talk, and then go on chopping. They worked until they had enough for four fires, and they covered each pile of wood with earth and built the fires. They finished well before sunset, so that there was still time for them to work a while planting kif. By the time it got dark they had sowed a good many rows of seeds.

The next day passed in the same way. The Djibli was content. At the end of the first week they had made so much charcoal that they needed six donkeys to carry it all. They loaded it and took it in to the Souq el Fham. The Rifi sold it for fourteen thousand francs. He gave five thousand to the Djibli, who was delighted. He was thinking of how he would be able to save it all, because he had no expenses at the Rifi's house.

Each day they cut down trees and each week they carried the charcoal to the market and sold it. Meanwhile the patch of kif was growing. The Rifi covered it carefully every night with three sheets of tarpaulin, and took them off the first thing each morning, so the leaves could get the early sun.

When summer came, the Rifi set to work picking his vegetables. Now the rains are finished, he told the Djibli, and there's no more work for you. But come back when it begins to rain next winter.

He gave a great many vegetables to the Djibli, as well as a load of charcoal and ten thousand francs.

The Djibli packed everything onto his donkey. Then he stood looking at the Rifi. And the kif? he said.

You can see when it'll be ripe. Come around and I'll give you your share, the Rifi told him.

The Djibli said good-bye and went home. But he was not happy, in spite of all the Rifi's gifts. He kept thinking of how hard he had worked there in Rehreh, and he felt certain that when the kif was ripe the Rifi would not keep his word.

I wonder how much he's going to get for all that kif, he thought. I'll never see any of it.

For several weeks the Djibli went on thinking about the kif. Finally he decided not to wait any longer. One night he started out for Rehreh on his donkey carrying a pail of creosote with him.

In the whole village there was not a light, but he knew every path. He went straight to the Rifi's kif patch and carefully spread the creosote over each plant. Then he covered everything again with the tarpaulins and rode back to the city.

Early in the morning the Rifi got up and went out to uncover the kif. His eyes grew large when he saw the dead plants shining with creosote. He stood a while looking, and the tears came out of his eyes.

Then he uprooted the kif and carried it to the edge of the stream, where he made a bonfire of it. He watched it until it all had burned. That day he dug up the topsoil in the kif patch and made a high pile of it, to get rid of all the creosote that had soaked into the earth. After that he spaded the dirt underneath and sowed more kif seeds. Before the day was finished he had planted a new kif patch.

This time he was even more careful of his young plants. He watered them very gently in the evening, and hurried to look at them several times each day, to be certain they were all right.

One afternoon the Djibli appeared in the field where the Rifi was working. Salaam aleikoum.

Aleikoum salaam.

They shook hands. How's everything? said

the Djibli. How's that kif? Isn't it ready yet?

The Rifi sighed. The kif! he said. It's gone. Some son of a whore came one night and poured tar over it all. I had to pull it up and burn it. But I've got some more growing, and it won't be long before it's ready. I'm making it grow fast. I'm only afraid of the dew at night. I have to cover it very early, before sunset, or it'll go black. Come and look. It's growing up healthy and tall.

He took the Djibli over to see the young plants. The Djibli stared at them for a moment. There are a lot of sons of whores around, he said.

Let's have some tea, said the Rifi. We can sit over there under the cypresses.

He made tea in the garden, and they took their glasses and sat on a mat in the shade. And they smoked their pipes and talked.

When they got up the Rifi said: It won't be long now before winter will be here. As soon as it begins to rain, you come back to work.

Good, said the Djibli.

The Rifi filled the panniers of the Djibli's donkey with vegetables, gave him two thousand francs, and they said good-bye.

When the Djibli had gone, the Rifi sprinkled his kif plants with water and gently spread the tarpaulins over them.

Behind the scrub where the kif was planted there was a path that led between the bushes down to the stream. One day when the Rifi stood looking at his kif, he saw a wild boar going along the path. This worried him. He went to the house and got a pick and shovel, and then he walked down toward the stream. At a place under the trees he began to dig, and he went on digging until he had made a trench about six feet deep.

All the next day he carried baskets full of broken bottles and old barbed wire and cactus, until the bed of the trench was full. After that he built a trellis of cane stalks and laid it over the top of the pit, and spread heavy paper over the canes. Then he covered it all with earth. All this took a long time. He ran back and forth for many hours. And each time he passed the patch of kif he looked at it.

If a boar walks just once through the kif it'll kill it, he thought. I've got to catch that boar. Besides, I can sell it to the Spaniards at Oued Bahrein.

Late one afternoon not long afterward, before the rains had begun, there was a knock at the Rifi's door. He opened it and found the Djibli standing there.

Msalkheir! I wasn't doing anything this evening, and I thought I'd come by and see you. I was wondering. Could you give me a few vegetables?

Yes, I think so, said the Rifi.

And the kif? How's it coming?

It's almost ripe, the Rifi told him. But there's not much of it this time. Come and look.

They walked together out to the kif patch. As the Djibli went along he was thinking: He won't give me any, that's certain. He'll find some excuse. He's already saying there isn't much.

After they had stood looking at the kif, they went back to the house and sat down. You'll eat with me, the Rifi said.

Later they drank tea and smoked kif. When it was time for the Djibli to start back to the city, the Rifi went out and got the vegetables for him. He filled one pannier with vegetables and the other with charcoal, gave the Djibli a thousand francs, and sent him riding down the road on his donkey.

All that day the Djibli had been thinking of the kif he had expected to carry back with him to the city. Now, without the kif, his head was full of poison for the Rifi. Before he got home he had already resolved to kill the new batch of kif as well.

On the way to his house he stopped at a café and bought a packet of kif. He went home and sat down to smoke, and he smoked pipe after pipe. Soon he got up and went out into the dark. With the pail of creosote he set out on the donkey again for Rehreh.

It seemed to him that the safest way of getting to the kif patch without being seen was to cross the stream and creep along the path behind the bushes. Once he had crossed the stream he jumped off the donkey. Leaving it there, he went up, along the path where the boar-trap was. When he walked onto the false earth over the pit, the cover broke with his weight, and he dropped down onto the bed of glass and cactus spikes.

The blood was running out of his body. Everyone was asleep, and there was no one to hear even his loudest cries, out there in the woods.

In the morning the Rifi got up and went out to take the covers off his kif. He looked closely at the plants, and found them all smiling and happy. He left them uncovered, waiting for the sun, and went to another part of the garden where his vegetables grew. Soon he decided to go down and see the boar-trap.

When he saw the open pit ahead of him in

the path, he smiled. He was sure he had caught the boar.

He leaned over, saw the Djibli, and ran to get a rope. He came back and slung the rope over a branch of one of the trees, making it secure with a noose. Then slowly he let himself down in. The Djibli was dead, covered with blood and creosote.

Then the Rifi knew who had destroyed his kif, and he realized that the boar had made it possible for him to kill the Djibli without any guilt. No one can foresee the plans of Allah, he murmured.

He climbed up and ran to his house. There he got out several kilos of lime for whitewashing, which he dumped into a cauldron full of water. He worked at it, mashing it and stirring it until it bubbled and steamed. He carried it down to the pit and poured it over the Djibli. Then he threw in rocks, and after that he shovelled in earth, until the pit was filled up. In the place where it had been he planted weeds and bushes. No sign remained that there ever had been a trench dug there.

From then on the Rifi lived alone and cut his trees alone. He picked his kif and smoked it by himself, and had no more trouble.

THE DOCTOR FROM THE CHEMEL

At the entrance to the Khalifa's palace there was a garden full of fountains and flowers. It was here that a certain Nchaioui used to come each day to sit under a fig tree. He would set his basket down and take from it a sheepskin which he always carried with him. Then he would spread out the sheepskin and sit on it. In the basket he also had charcoal, a teapot, and a bowl of majoun. He would place three stones in such a way that there was room between them to make a fire, set the teapot on top, and wait for the water to boil. Any day you could see him sitting there in the garden on the sheepskin. He had no work, but he had many friends who kept him alive with small sums of money which they gave him from time to time.

It became known that the Khalifa was suffering from an abscess in a private part of his body, and that as a result he could not sit down. The best doctors had been called, but they were not able to help him. The reason for this was that the Khalifa, being ashamed, would not let them examine the abscess. He called in holy men and tolba who chanted the Koran for him, but the pain went on.

The Nchaioui heard about the Khalifa's difficulties, and straightway he went to the garden and began to eat majoun. He ate more than usual that day, and smoked a great deal of kif as well. All the while he was thinking about the Khalifa. When he was feeling happy, he lay back in the shade of the fig tree and said to himself: I think I can cure him.

Soon he rose, folded his sheepskin, put his pipe and teapot and bowl of majoun into the basket, and went to knock at the Khalifa's gate. A Sudanese opened it and asked him what he wanted.

I'm a doctor, he said.

Where are you from? said the black man, looking at his ragged robes. We've had all the doctors in the country.

I'm from the Chemel, he told him. I've got medicines that will make anybody feel better, no matter how sick he is.

Wait, said the black man. I'll be back in a while.

The Sudanese went in to his master's chamber and told him that a toubib had arrived from the Chemel.

The Khalifa was lying on his belly. He raised his head a little and sighed. Bring him in, he said.

The servant went to the gate. Come with me, he told the Nchaioui.

In the chamber the Nchaioui saw the Khalifa lying face down on the bed. Bring plenty of honey and hot tea, he told the black man, and he sat down on the bed beside the Khalifa.

When the servant returned with the tea and honey, the Nchaioui took out his bowl and scooped up a large ball of majoun, which he handed to the Khalifa. First eat this, he told him. And drink this tea afterward.

The Khalifa did as he was told, and the Nchaioui kept giving him more tea to drink. When an hour had passed, and the Nchaioui saw that the majoun had taken effect, he sent the servant out of the room and stood up.

This is the moment for the medicine, he said. He reached down and pulled off the Khalifa's tchamir, leaving his buttocks uncovered. The Khalifa did not even notice.

Then the Nchaioui anointed his sex with honey and thrust it with great force into the Khalifa.

The Khalifa uttered a scream, and tried to throw the Nchaioui off, but he did not have the strength. After that he was quiet while the Nchaioui worked.

The operation is almost over, your Excel-

21

lency, said the Nchaioui. He finished and withdrew his sex, very much pleased. The abscess had burst, and he summoned the black man and told him to bring towels and clean his master.

Meanwhile the Khalifa, who had been in pain for a long time, was so relieved by the bursting of the abscess that he fell asleep. Seeing this, the Nchaioui unrolled his sheepskin and lay down on it at the foot of the bed. In the morning when he awoke, he found the Khalifa still sleeping.

The Khalifa awoke shortly afterward, and the Nchaioui helped him out of bed.

I have no more pain, said the Khalifa.

Hamdoul'lah! said the Nchaioui.

Together they went into the Khalifa's bathing chambers. After the servants had poured water over them and gone out, the Khalifa said: Last night, when you operated on me, what did you use? A pole of some kind?

Your Excellency, I used this. He pointed at his sex.

What? cried the Khalifa. But that means you assaulted me. You assaulted your Khalifa!

No, your Excellency, I operated on you, nothing more.

Good, said the Khalifa, remembering that

the Nchaioui had indeed cured him.

They came out of the hamman, and the Khalifa ordered a great festival to be given immediately. There were musicians and dancers, and the guests ate and drank tea for many hours. In the middle of the party the Nchaioui took out his bowl of majoun and gave a spoonful to the Khalifa. Soon the Khalifa began to talk and laugh and sing, and the Nchaioui knew that he was happy. He put everything into his basket and stood up.

I must leave, your Excellency, he said.

How much do I owe you? the Khalifa asked him.

Sidi, whatever you give me will be more than enough, because it comes from you.

He is a great doctor, thought the Khalifa. He sent a servant for a pouch full of dinars, and gave it to him.

The Nchaioui thanked him and left. Then he went across the street and sat under the fig tree to smoke kif.

THE YOUNG MAN WHO LIVED ALONE

A man named Si Quaddour had been left a large tract of land by his father. There was a big house at one end of it where the family lived, and a half mile or so from the house there was a grove of trees. Here in the shade at the edge of a stream Si Quaddour's father had built a small house and arranged a garden around it. The old man had spent most of his time sitting in this garden, far from his family.

Si Quaddour was a busy man, and never went near the little house in the woods. His son, however, a youth of seventeen, liked to smoke kif, and his grandfather's garden seemed to him the perfect place to do it. He began to spend more and more time there, until finally he moved out of his family's house altogether and went to live alone in the woods. Once a month he would go into the town and buy what he needed, such as matches, or a new pipe, or more kif. Each afternoon he walked to his father's house and got the food he would be eating that night and the next day.

His grandfather had made a pool in the garden, and it was beside the pool that the young man liked to sit. He would stay without moving for long periods of time, so that the birds would come and light near him. He had spent many months trying to become their friend. It took patience and intelligence, and a good deal of kif besides, to learn how to sit as he did, waiting for the birds to come. But usually they came, and sometimes they even perched on his shoulder. And it seemed to him that they were trying to talk to him, as if they believed he understood what they were saying with their chirping.

One day a group of relatives from another part of the country arrived to call on Si Quaddour and his family. Among them there was a young mute girl. She sat with the rest of the family for a while, and then, growing restless, she got up and wandered outside. The orchards were beautiful, and so she took a walk. After a while she came to the grove of trees, and the path led her to the small house by the river.

As she went into the garden she saw the youth sitting by the pool with two birds on the ground in front of him. He seemed to be talking to them. The girl stood still, and her mouth opened in astonishment. The birds were chirping very loud. The young man listened, and appeared to be saying something to them. He raised his arms and the two birds flew away.

Then he began to laugh. At that moment he looked up and saw the girl watching him from the other end of the garden. It seemed to him that he had never seen such a beautiful face.

He called to her: Who are you?

The girl put her hand in front of her mouth and shrugged her shoulders, to say that she could not speak. He went over to her and made gestures, and she showed that she understood.

What are you doing way out here in the woods? he wanted to know.

She made signs to say that her family were visiting at a big house beyond the orchards, and he told her it was his father's house.

He led the girl to the pool and told her to sit down. Then he made her some tea. As she drank he filled his pipe with kif and lighted it. He poured himself a glass of tea and sat smoking and looking at her.

The girl was making a great effort to say something to him, but he raised his hand and said: No. Don't try to talk. I want to dream a little.

They were both silent for a while, as the kif climbed into the young man's head and he listened to the sound of the river flowing by.

After a time he rose and said to the girl:

Come with me. I'll show you the way back to my father's house.

They started to walk through the woods. He talked to her, and she answered by moving her hands. Suddenly a snake rose up in the middle of the path, as if it were going to strike at them. The girl saw it, and her fear was so great that she opened her mouth and screamed with all her force. The fear had loosened her voice.

The snake went to one side, and lay among the leaves by the edge of the path.

I speak now, said the girl. The youth looked at her, but he did not understand.

Soon he told her: Now we're out of the grove. And you can see the house up there. Just keep going.

Yes, she said, and she went on to the house, thinking: Now I can speak.

The young man turned around and went back to where the snake was waiting for him. He stopped and ran his hand along its back two or three times, and it slid away. Then he walked on to his garden and sat smoking kif by the pool.

HASSAN AND THE AGHREBIA

Hassan was not married. He was a kif-smoker, and liked freedom. His closest friend was an old man named Si Mokhtar, whom he had known since boyhood.

One day Si Mokhtar stopped at Hassan's house to see him. Hassan had him sit down on the mattress, and he made a fire so he could invite him to dinner. While the food was cooking, they smoked a few pipes of kif.

After they had eaten, they drank tea and smoked more kif. As they were talking, Hassan said: Si Mokhtar, it's hard to believe you're seventy-five years old. You're strong. You seem a lot younger. Look at me. I'm thirty-five, and I'm no good for anything.

People aren't all alike, you know, my son. You're you and I'm me, and each one is himself.

Yes, of course, said Hassan.

I'm me and I take care of myself, the old man said. You don't take care of yourself at all.

That's true, Si Mokhtar. I've never bothered, and now it's too late. Last night I had a girl with me. I spent the whole night with her, waiting. I couldn't do anything. She kissed me. She hugged me. She did everything. But nothing could wake it up. It went right on sleeping.

Si Mokhtar began to laugh. This must be the first time it's happened to you, or you wouldn't be so worried, he told Hassan. That happens to everybody. You just take a little aghrebia.

Aghrebia? Have you got some?

No. I don't need it, said the old man, and he winked at Hassan.

Where do I buy it?

Si Mokhtar shook his head. They don't sell it, my son.

Hassan looked unhappy.

If you want some, I can tell you how to make it yourself, Si Mokhtar went on. And when you've made it, you bring it here to me, and I'll tell you what to do with it.

Of course I want some. What do I do?

First you get some kharouah beans and boil them until the water's black. Then you dry them out in a skillet over the fire. Don't throw the black water out. You've got to have a lot of other things ready, like flour and eggs and sugar and nuts and spices.

And Si Mokhtar went on to explain to Hassan how to make aghrebia. When you take it to the bakery, tell the maallem not to leave it in the oven more than a half hour, he said.

Tomorrow, incha'Allah, I'll make the medicine, and you can come and see it.

Si Mokhtar agreed. Presently he got up and went out.

Early in the morning Hassan got up and gathered the kharouah beans from a plant along the road. He took them home and put them on to boil. After that he went out and bought all the other things he needed. He made the dough into pellets, as Si Mokhtar had told him to do, and took them out to the oven. Then he waited a half hour while they were being baked.

He found Si Mokhtar sitting in the café where he always sat. He sat down and ordered a glass of coffee. They began to smoke their kif pipes.

I've made the medicine, said Hassan.

Good, said Si Mokhtar.

Soon they got up and went to Hassan's house. Hassan showed the old man the pellets, and Si Mokhtar said: Yes. That's the way they looked when I used to make them. And he took a knife and cut one of the pellets in half.

Eat this, he said. And now drink a glass of hot tea.

Hassan did as he was told.

Half an hour or so later Hassan began to sweat. He shut his eyes, and it seemed to him that he heard sounds such as he had never heard. And things he had never before seen passed in front of his eyes. He was sure he was floating through the air.

Soon Si Mokhtar asked him how he felt.

Ah, said Hassan. I don't believe in the world. There's another world where life is different.

I told you, said Si Mokhtar.

I didn't think you were lying. Anyway, I feel wonderful.

A little later the blood began to fill Hassan's sex, and it awoke. Si Mokhtar noticed this. Again he asked him how he felt.

Still better, Hassan said.

I must go, said Si Mokhtar, getting up.

Take some of the medicine with you, Hassan told him. The old man picked up three of the pellets and put them into the hood of his djellaba. Then he went out.

When Hassan went to bed that night, he did not feel at all sleepy. Soon he got up, put on his clothes, and went out to the Zoco Chico. As he walked by the Café Central he looked in and saw a young American girl sitting alone. He went in and sat down at the next table. Then he started to talk to the girl, and she answered him.

He moved to her table, and they talked for a

while. Soon he took out his kif pipe, filled it, and handed it to her. She smoked it and smiled. They each had a coffee. When Hassan asked her if she wanted to go home with him, she said it was all right, only she had to go to her hotel first.

Hassan paid and they walked to her hotel, a small, dark, very dirty place not far from the Zoco Chico. He went upstairs with her and she opened the door. There was a young man lying on the bed.

This is my friend, the girl said. Can he come too?

Hassan was certain that if he said no, she would not go with him, and so he said: Of course. But he was already thinking of how he could get rid of the young man. He looked again at him. He had long golden hair like a girl and wore many strings of beads and strange things around his neck.

The three of them started out for Hassan's house. When they got there, Hassan made them sit down, and then he put the water on to boil for tea.

The pellets of aghrebia were in a dish on the table, and the girl and her friend were looking at them. Are those hashish cakes? she wanted to know.

That's aghrebia. Try some.

Hassan gave her half a cake, and she ate it. Then she reached out and took another half. By the time he saw what was happening she had swallowed it. Since it was too late, he did not say anything. He tried to put the dish away, but the young man wanted a pellet. Hassan gave him one.

They drank their tea. About twenty minutes later Hassan saw that the girl's eyes were almost shut and that she was sweating. He looked at the young man to see if he had noticed it, and saw that he too was feeling the effects of the medicine.

Are you all right? he asked them.

I feel marvelous! the girl said. There's nowhere anything like the place I'm in right now. I can hear the air blowing by me like music, like music that could never be in the world. I'm not connected to the earth at all. I'm in the sky! In the sky!

You're right, you're right, said Hassan. That's the way it is.

The young man merely sat smiling, with his eyes shut. The girl ran her fingers through his long hair, and told Hassan: My friend feels the same as I do. He's in the sky, too.

Then she spoke to the boy in their own language, and he turned and kissed her without opening his eyes.

Hassan picked up the plate of aghrebia and handed it to the young man, thinking that if he could get him to take more he might make him lose consciousness. But the young man opened his eyes, saw the dish and shook his head, without letting go of the girl. And as Hassan sat there, not believing his eyes, the two Americans took off each other's clothing and began to make love on his bed in front of him. He was too astonished to move from where he sat, and he could not say a word. Then he jumped up and climbed the stairs to the roof, where he walked back and forth for an hour or more. When he went downstairs again the two Americans had their clothes on and were sitting on the bed looking at one another. He opened the door, and they got up and wandered out into the street. Then he slammed the door shut and bolted it.

The next day at the café, Hassan found Si Mokhtar in a very good humor. I had a girl with me all night, the old man told him. I took a little of your aghrebia. And he began to tell him about his night.

Soon he saw that Hassan was not listening, and so he did not talk about it any more.

THE SEA IN THE STREET

A certain kif-smoker got up one morning, had breakfast with his wife, and then began to smoke kif mixed with qoqa. His wife, seeing what he was doing, objected, saying: Why don't you smoke tobacco in the morning and leave kif and qoqa until the afternoon at least? You haven't even gone to market yet.

But he said he was only going to smoke a pipe or two before he went to the market. He smoked two pipes and got up and went out. He bought the vegetables for the day, and everything that he and his wife needed. Finally he went to the fish market, where an old friend of his had a stall. They greeted one another, and slapped each other on the back.

How's your kif today? asked the fish-seller, who had none in his stall with him.

My kif is always number one, said the man. I cut it myself every day.

Fill me a pipe, will you?

The man filled his sebsi and the fish-seller smoked it. Come inside, he said. I've got some hot tea for you.

The man stepped inside the stall and sat down, and his friend poured him a glass of tea. They sat for an hour or so, talking and smoking and sipping the tea. Then the man bought a kilo of swordfish, paid for it, and went home, his head singing with the kif he had smoked.

His wife opened the door. You were so long, she said. Lunch is going to be very late today.

Think of it, he said. I met a man I hadn't seen in years. We began to talk, and it got late. Are you hungry?

I ate a little, she said.

Here's the food. He spread it out. Why don't you cook it?

Where's the oil? You didn't bring any oil.

Give me a bottle and I'll go and get it, he told her.

She brought him an old French wine-bottle with a deep depression in the bottom. He took it and went out to a shop not far away.

The bacal was behind the counter, holding his kif pipe in his hand, being just about to light it. Instead, he greeted the man and handed him the pipe. The man smoked it and sat down on a crate inside the doorway. He filled the pipe and passed it back to the bacal. Give me a limonada, he told him. I'm thirsty.

The bacal opened two bottles of limonada, and they began to smoke and talk together. The empty wine-bottle lay on the floor, and the wife went on waiting for the oil.

She sat a while, and then she grew tired of waiting. She decided to go to a neighbor's house to borrow the oil. When she got back home she waited a while longer. Finally she was so hungry that she cooked the fish and ate it.

The man went on sitting with the bacal, talking and laughing. When customers came in, the bacal would wait on them, and the man would fill his pipe and smoke while he waited for the bacal to sit down again.

It grew dark. Suddenly the man looked up and cried out.

What's the matter? said the bacal.

Give me a liter of oil, he told him. My wife's waiting for it. He handed the bottle to the bacal, who filled a liter measure and began to pour the oil into the bottle. Soon the bottle was full, but because of the false bottom, there was still a good deal of oil in the measure.

You've got some more here, the bacal said. Where do you want me to put it?

The man stood for a moment looking at the bottle in his hand. Then he felt the depression in the bottom, and turned the bottle upside down.

Here, he said, showing the depression to the bacal. Pour it in here.

The bacal stared at him, and at the oil which was running all over the counter and onto the floor. Then, having a great deal of kif in his head, he poured what was left of the oil into the depression in the bottom of the bottle.

The man paid him, said good-bye, and went out of the shop. It was evening, and the east wind had risen a little. As he stepped into the open and felt the fresh air inside him, all the kif he had smoked suddenly blossomed in his brain.

He came to the street where he lived, and stood still, looking at the street stretching away from him into the distance. Instead of the street, he saw the sea, with high waves rolling toward him in the moonlight.

What a sea! he thought, and he shrugged. He took off his jacket and trousers, and his shirt and his underwear. When he was naked, he carefully wrapped the bottle of oil inside his clothing, and tied the bundle to the top of his head so that he could swim. Then he gave a great leap and plunged into the waves.

He landed on his belly at the base of a cactus fence, where there were piles of excrement. Strong waves, he thought, and he kept crawling along the street as if he were swimming, until he reached the door of his house.

Then he got to his feet and pounded on the door.

When his wife saw him naked, bloody, and smeared with excrement, her mouth fell open and she could say nothing.

Can't you see? he cried. The ocean has come. Look at the size of those waves out there!

She grabbed him and pulled him inside and slammed the door. Then she pushed him into the latrine and gave him a bath with many pails of water which she dashed over him. After that she dried him off and put him to bed.

In the middle of the night he began to call out to his wife: I've brought the oil! You can cook the fish now. I'm hungry.

TWO FRIENDS AND THE RAIN

Two friends, Farid and Mansour, had stalls side by side in the market. Since they both liked to smoke kif and eat hashish, they decided to live together. They found themselves a house with only one room. They had a reed mat, a small table, a chest, a brazier and one cooking pot. They made their tea in a tin can. But they had two mattresses, one for each, and each mattress had its own blanket.

One rainy night in the middle of winter, they ate a big tajine of lamb and quinces. Afterwards, content with the food inside them, they lay back, each on his mattress, and smoked many pipes of kif. Soon Farid rose and brought out a bar of hashish.

It was raining very hard, and the wind was shaking the house. They sat for a long time, nibbling on the hashish and listening to the rain. Finally Mansour turned out the light and they both shut their eyes and began to travel toward other worlds.

The rain kept falling, and the sound it made grew louder. It was very dark in the room. Soon the noise was so great that Farid returned from where he had been.

What a storm! he said. Listen to that rain.

That, my friend, is not rain, Mansour told him.

It's not? What is it, then?

It's water.

Farid laughed. But Mansour said: There is nothing to laugh at. They're not the same thing. Rain is rain, and water's water. And that's water falling onto our roof.

I've got to get some sleep, said Farid. I can't talk all night.

It was you who started, said Mansour.

They were quiet. The storm grew worse. Mansour lay on his back. He was almost asleep. It was then that the roof sprang a leak. At first there was only a drop now and then. It fell directly onto his left eyelid. But soon it began to drip faster. And the drops spattered onto his eyelids, and ran down his face and neck. He tried to travel toward other worlds again, but the rain kept him nailed to his mattress.

He called out finally. Farid!

Farid only groaned.

Farid! Do me a big favor. Come over here and move my head a little. The water's falling into my eyes.

Farid groaned again.

Then Mansour said: What's the matter with you?

There's a rat on my pillow, and every little while he starts to bite my ear. Couldn't you take the cane and get rid of him?

Mansour lay still. What a storm! he sighed. The rain went on dripping into his face, and soon he was asleep.

When the rat finally drove its teeth through the lobe of his ear, Farid managed to move his hand and drive it away. Then he too fell asleep.

THE DATURA TREES

There were two young friends, Hamed and Mustafa, who had been living together for several years. They had a three-room house, and each one paid half the rent. They both worked in the Fondouk ech Chijra weaving rugs. In the evening when they had finished their work, they went together to a café or a cinema, and then they went home. Whatever they did, they did together.

Mustafa, however, had once lived in Casablanca, and he still had friends there. One of these was a boy named Abdeslam whom he had not seen in two years, but who suddenly wrote him a letter saying that he would like to visit him in Tangier.

Mustafa knew that Hamed could not get on with the people of Casablanca, and so he spoke of the letter to him, to see what Hamed would say. He was not sure that Hamed would agree to having Abdeslam in the house.

Hamed only shrugged and said: He's coming to see you, not me. Mustafa decided that it would be all right to tell Abdeslam to come. He wanted very much to see him.

The day Abdeslam was due to arrive, they went down to the beach and waited for the bus to come in. When it drew up, Abdeslam was the first one out. He jumped down and hugged Mustafa and kissed him on both cheeks.

Abdeslam, this is Hamed, my friend.

Hamed and Abdeslam shook hands. They all got into a taxi and went to the house.

There Mustafa made tea for Abdeslam, while Hamed went out to the market to buy food for dinner. When he came back, he sat down and had tea with them. He took out his sebsi, and they began to smoke.

After they had talked a while, Mustafa could see that Hamed did not like Abdeslam at all, and he hoped there would be no trouble. It was not long before Mustafa got up and went out to buy a pack of cigarettes. When he came back he found the two glaring at one another angrily, and he felt that if he had come a moment later they would already have been fighting. However, they went on talking, and soon Hamed went out into the kitchen to cook the dinner. When it was ready, he brought it into the room and set it on the taifor. Then he cut the bread.

The three friends sat down to eat, but Hamed was not hungry. He could not swallow his food. He felt that inside him everything was shut off.

Hurry and finish, he told the others. I'm invited to the Marshan to see some Americans, and you're coming with me.

When the meal was over, they took a taxi up the hill to the Marshan. There were lights in the garden around the house. Hamed rang a bell, and an American with a glass in his hand came and unlocked the gate.

He introduced Mustafa and Abdeslam to the American.

In one room several Americans were sitting with their feet up on the tables, drinking and laughing. The three guests shook hands with all of them and sat down in a row together on a couch.

Hamed was sitting next to the door that led into the garden behind the house. He looked out at the trees and saw several large daturas there, with hundreds of big white flowers hanging down from their branches.

The American came in with pastries and coffee for the three friends, since they did not drink whiskey like the others. Hamed took out his sebsi and smoked four or five pipes of kif. After that he began to stare more intently into the garden. He was thinking of the insults Abdeslam had given him while Mustafa had been buying cigarettes.

He sat looking steadily out into the garden where the breeze made the shadows move in the leaves, and it seemed to him that behind the trees he saw the form of a woman. She was wearing a white haïk, and she was waving to him.

He set the kif pipe on the table and stood up. Mustafa stared at him, seeing the expression on his face, and watched him as he walked slowly out into the garden.

Hamed never looked away from the spot where he had seen the woman. When he was under the datura trees he stood still for a long time, looking into the shadows where he knew she was standing. The white flowers gave off a strong, sweet smell.

After a while Hamed's American friend came out to see what he was doing alone in the garden for such a long time. Hamed did not realize that the man was there until he touched his shoulder. Then he jumped.

What's the matter? said the American.

Nothing. You startled me.

You look strange. What's happened?

Hamed turned around, shook his head slowly, and said in a low voice: I never knew my mother. Then he began to walk toward the door.

He sat down beside Mustafa for a while and listened to the Americans talking and laughing. After a while he got up again and wandered out into the garden. This time he stood under one of the trees and picked six of the white flowers. He stuffed them into his pocket. The American saw him from the doorway, and as he came in he asked him: Won't the flowers get all crumpled up in your pocket?

It doesn't matter, Hamed said. I like to have them there because they smell good.

The American laughed, and Hamed went in and sat down. Soon he said to Mustafa: Let's go.

Mustafa and Abdeslam stood up. They all shook hands with everyone, and went out.

When they got home, Mustafa and Abdeslam sat down together and went on talking. Hamed said he was going to make some coffee. They looked up and said they would like some. He went into the kitchen. Taking the flowers out of his pocket, he dropped them into the pot of water. He stood for a good while watching them as they boiled. Then he took them out and threw them down the latrine. He used the yellow water in which they had been boiling to make the coffee, and he made it very strong. When it was ready, he filled two glasses and took them into the other room. Then he went into the kitchen and got his own coffee, and sat down with them.

Mustafa and Abdeslam drank the coffee as they talked. They went on talking, but it was not long before their words began to come out very slowly. And there were long silences between them, until finally Mustafa shut his eyes and rolled over with his head on the floor. Abdeslam stayed where he was, with his eyes and mouth open, but he did not move at all. It was as if he had been made of stone.

Hamed sat down beside Abdeslam, reached out, and unfastened Abdeslam's belt. He began to pull down his trousers. Abdeslam did not move. He got the trousers off, and then he pulled off Abdeslam's shorts as well. Still he did not move. Hamed pushed him and rolled him over onto his belly. He knelt above him and spat between his buttocks. Then he made him pay for the insults, as the woman under the datura trees had told him to do. When he had finished he went into his room and slept.

In the morning he arose and made his breakfast. Soon Mustafa awoke, and got up off the floor where he had been all night. Then he saw Abdeslam lying there, just as Hamed had left him the night before, with his buttocks still uncovered. He looked at Hamed without speaking.

Yes, I did it, said Hamed. I swore to my mother I'd do it, and I did it. I've got to go out. When your friend wakes up, you watch him. He's going to put his hand back there. Then he's going to look at you, and put on his pants fast, and go down to the beach and take a bus for Casablanca. I'll see you later.

ALLAH'S WORDS

Si Brahim was a very religious man. He was so fond of the Koran that he imagined other people did not hold it in high enough esteem, and he often felt it his duty to counsel his friends and neighbors against ordinary sins such as stealing, buggery and drunkenness. He also gave generously to the poor. A good man, people said when he passed by. Like a saint, said some. They kissed his hand and called him Cherif.

Si Brahim owned a big bazaar where many tourists came each day to buy things. He had a son who was nearly twenty, and it was the young man whom Si Brahim left in charge of the bazaar when he went to pray at the mosque. When he heard the words of the Koran being chanted, he always felt that life was good. Sometimes he would stay in the mosque all day long, seated in a dark corner on a mat, merely listening to the words. He knew that most people could not afford this luxury, and yet he thought it would be a wonderful thing if others could hear the holy words all day long, the way it was his own good fortune to be able to do.

He reflected on this, and one day he went to

a Hindu shop and bought a large tape-recorder. That night he told his son that he had decided to make a gift to the neighborhood. I want you to fill this tape with words from the Koran, he told him.

The young man took the tape to his room and kept it there for a week or so, until he had filled it with surat from the Koran. Then he gave it back to his father.

Si Brahim set the loudspeakers up in the window, and started the machine going, so that the people in the street below could hear Allah's words. It made him very happy to hear them so loud and strong, and he was delighted with his idea. The passers-by were pleased, too. They called up to him: May Allah prolong your life!

Si Brahim sat happily in the window the rest of the day, playing the tape over and over. The following day he stayed only an hour or so at the bazaar, prayed quickly at the mosque, and went home to continue working for the neighbors with the machine.

The third day his wife came in as he was sitting there in the window, and said: Are you just going to be sitting there playing that machine from now on?

Si Brahim was indignant. I'm giving people

the words of Allah, woman, he said.

Can't we have a little quiet? What's the matter with you? And she went out of the room angrily.

After a few days Si Brahim noticed that the people no longer seemed to be stopping to listen to the words he was playing for them, nor did anyone call up blessings upon him. This was only because they had heard enough of the loud words coming from the window. Many of them in the quarter now thought Si Brahim a little crazy. His family came to know of this, and were very much ashamed. But there was nothing they could do about it. The son comforted his mother. I'll try and think of something, he told her.

Si Brahim went on sitting in his window, thinking: They're not listening. They don't want to hear the words of Allah. One day he could stand it no longer, and he went down into the street and began to stop the passers-by.

Do you hear those words? he cried. Then why don't you pay attention to them? They're the words of God. And you're not living the way they tell you to live.

And the people began to say: You see? He's getting worse. They shook their heads and clicked their tongues. Si Brahim heard them, and he was very much upset. He could not eat his lunch that day, and he went out to sit in a café.

After he had gone, his son decided to go and see a friend of his, a young man who also had a tape-recorder. He persuaded him to go with him to his house and to bring the machine along with him. There they placed the two machines together and rerecorded all the words of the Koran that were on the tape, but backwards. When they had finished, they put the new tape onto Si Brahim's machine and went into the next room where the rest of the family were having tea.

At the café Si Brahim met a friend whom he had known for many years. The man was now a heavy kif-smoker. They sat together talking for a while, and the friend offered Si Brahim some kif.

No. I never smoke it, Si Brahim said.

That's too bad. You might not look so sad if you did.

Si Brahim did not answer. After a moment he said: You must come and have dinner with me at my house.

Good, said the man.

I'll play you the words of Allah on my tape-recorder, Si Brahim told him. He thought this might be good for the kif-smoker.

The man had heard about Si Brahim's tape-recorder from the people who lived in the quarter. Ouakha, he said.

They paid the qahouaji and set off for Si Brahim's house. As they went in, Si Brahim was saying: People don't want to hear the words of Allah any more.

His son met them at the door and went into the room with them. When his father was not looking, he winked at the visitor.

The two men sat down. Si Brahim called his wife and asked for tea, and said that his friend would be staying for dinner. The woman went back to the family and told them: He's brought that old hacheichi home for dinner. It's the only way he can get anybody to listen to his machine. I feel sorry for the poor hacheichi.

Meanwhile Si Brahim got up and went over to his tape-recorder. He started to play the tape, and the words that came out sounded like frogs trying to speak. His mouth opened in surprise, and he stopped the machine and changed the speed. Then it sounded like birds chirping. He changed it back again and listened, but he could not understand a word that was coming from it. He shook his head and was about to turn the machine off.

What's the matter? said his friend. Let me hear it.

Si Brahim looked at the man, and decided that his head was full of kif. He shut off the tape-recorder. There's something wrong with it, he said. It's not playing right.

Leave it alone, the man told him. Why did you shut it off? Open it up and let it play. You invited me here to listen to Allah's words. Let me listen.

He understood that Si Brahim's son was playing a joke of some sort on his father, and so he decided to play too. Si Brahim started the machine going once again, and his friend said: Good. Now come and sit down. I'll fill you a pipe and we can listen.

Si Brahim was so upset and confused that he took the pipe and smoked it. And each time his friend passed it to him he took it, and they went on listening to the noises coming out of the machine. By the time the tape was halfway through, the kif was singing in Si Brahim's head. He thought that perhaps he was beginning to understand the sounds coming from the tape. From time to time the family would peer between the curtains into the room and see the two men sitting there, and they would turn away quickly to hide their laughter.

When the tape had finished playing, Si

Brahim turned to his friend and said: Did you understand anything?

Understand? Of course. Didn't you?

Si Brahim scratched his chin. Not all of it, he said. The machine's not working right today.

It's a fine machine. It's working perfectly. I understood everything, his friend told him.

Then Si Brahim heard his family laughing in the next room. His wife was saying: Maybe this will teach him a lesson, and we can have a little peace at last.

By now Si Brahim's head was bursting with kif, and he misunderstood his wife's words, thinking she was complaining because he had smoked kif. He was very angry.

He got up and went to the door. You're wrong! he cried. I'm going to smoke whenever I want. And I'm going to learn how to cut the kif myself so that I can have it fresh every day. How do you like that, woman?

His friend was delighted to hear him saying this. When dinner was over he took Si Brahim back to the café, and they smoked until very late.

From then on Si Brahim spent all his time in cafés cutting and smoking kif. He was no longer interested in his tape-recorder, and so he gave it to his son.

THE KIF-CUTTER'S STORY

When I had no job and nothing at all to do, I cut kif. It was the only way I could find to make any money. I'd sit in this café out in Beni Makada and clean the plants, bunch by bunch, and when the café filled up with smokers I sold it to them. In small packages, as much or as little as they wanted. Some liked it with a lot of tobacco and some liked it lighter. Because I knew how to make good kif, and I was making it for real smokers. They wouldn't have bought it if it hadn't been good. I used only the best part of the plant.

One day I'd just finished cutting, and I was playing a game of ronda with some friends. I had a leaf of tobacco left over, and I'd left it lying on the table. I was going to put it away later. Pretty soon a man walked into the café. A man with a turban and djellaba, and yellow slippers on his feet and a cane in his hand, like a Djibli. We looked at him and he sat down and ordered a Coca Cola, and paid the qahouaji, and we went on playing. And then he reached out and picked up my leaf of tobacco and looked at it, and said: Whose is this?

I told him it was mine, and he said he wanted

to talk with me outside.

Where?

Outside.

All right. I got up and went out with him.

He had a car out there.

Get in, he says.

Who are you?

I'm from the Régie des Tabacs.

I get into the car and we drive to his office. There are three Frenchmen sitting there. And four Moroccans.

What's this one been doing? they say.

I found him sitting in a café. With this leaf of tobacco. The Djibli shakes the leaf up and down.

One of the Frenchmen turns to me. He speaks Arabic. Do you smoke kif?

I tell him if somebody offers me some I smoke it. I tell him I usually smoke tobacco.

And this leaf. Where did you get it? he wants to know.

There was a man came into the café this morning. I never saw him before, I tell him. He cut his kif and when he was finished he had a leaf left over. I asked him if I could have it and he said to take it.

And what did you want of it? he says.

I tell him there are lots of men who smoke

kif, and once in a while when they're cutting they need a little more tobacco. And I can help them out.

And you don't know it's a crime? *C'est défendu, ça!* Then he begins to shake the leaf in my face.

Non, monsieur, I tell him. I thought it was alcohol that was forbidden for Moslems, not tobacco. Anyway, it's just one leaf, and I don't even know who it belongs to.

They take me out with them and put me into the car again, and drive me to a dungeon they used to have out there behind the barracks at Beni Makada. Six days there in the dark. No place to sleep except on the floor. And the floor's made of stone. After six whole days and nights they come again and open the door and tell me to come out. So I go out and they drive me up to the office again.

The Frenchman is looking at me, and he says they're going to let me off this time. Only I've got to pay a fine of five hundred pesetas.

Why? For a leaf of tobacco? I tell him you can buy a whole kilo for two hundred pesetas, and he's charging me five hundred for one leaf?

You'll pay it or you'll stay five months in jail, he says.

I'll pay, I tell him. Six days is enough.

I pay him the five hundred and he tells me to go on home.

At home the whole family begins asking me where I've been. I told them I'd been to Tetuan, so as not to worry them. I bathed and changed my clothes, and went to the café.

When I went in, the others all said: That was a low trick they played on you. They shouldn't do such things to people.

Nothing happened, I told them. And later that day I went out and bought two kilos of kif and brought it back to the café. There I got up onto the musician's platform and spread it all out. I had three friends sitting around me, helping me get it ready fast. I called to the qahouaji and asked for four glasses of tea. I wanted them all to be in a good mood and work fast, so I gave them kif, and they smoked as they worked. While they were busy with the kif I got the tobacco ready. We finished at the same time, and then I began to cut. By the time the customers came in, it was all ready, so I didn't lose that day, at least.

In those times I could get a kilo of kif for a hundred and fifty pesetas. And a hundred more would buy a kilo of tobacco. I usually made about six hundred pesetas on a kilo of kif. But sometimes there was practically no kif in the city. I'd have none to sell and I'd be looking everywhere for it.

Once I went down to Emsallah on my bicycle to see a man who sometimes sold it to me. When I got near his house I saw a crowd of people outside. And then I saw the men from the Régie des Tabacs. I stood still and watched them bring out four sacks of kif, a hundred kilos each. And they carried out two hundred kilos of tobacco. The man and his brother were handcuffed. And there were two others with them. They piled the men and the kif and the tobacco into the truck and drove away. I felt sorry for them. It meant that each man would be five years in jail, and they would burn the kif and the tobacco. I felt sorry about all of it.

I went on to Tchar ej Jdid to see another man. He said the kif he had wasn't very good, but it was better than nothing. And tobacco? I asked him.

He said it was the best he could get. You can't get good kif or good tobacco either right now, he said. No matter how they try to bring it in, in a truck or a car, on a donkey or a bicycle, the gendarmes stop them and find it.

He wanted a hundred and fifty pesetas a

kilo for it, and I bought five kilos, and a kilo and a half of tobacco. I put it into my beach bag, strapped the bag to the back of my bicycle, and started off. Then I noticed a car with two men in it behind me. Whichever street I took, the car stayed behind me. My heart began to go fast. I was sure they were from the Régie des Tabacs. I turned to the left and coasted down a steep hill, and the car turned too. I was looking out for an alley that would be too narrow for the car to get into, but wide enough for the bicycle. I kept going along, and they came on behind slowly.

I was still looking for an alley when I got to Val Flores. Then I saw a path leading down to the river, and I rode along it fast, and lost the car, and kept going until I was behind the poorhouse. Then I coasted on down to the bakery. I stopped and gave the beach bag to the baker, and got back onto the bicycle and rode around for a half hour or so, and then went back to the oven. The baker had taken the sack of kif out of the bag, filled another sack like it with ends of bread, and slipped it back into the beach bag. He gave it to me and I strapped it on to the bicycle and started out for the café.

Just as I'm getting to the café, the car with

the two men drives up. I start to go in, but they begin yelling: Come here!

I just turn my head and look at them, and keep going.

They go on shouting.

I don't answer, and go into the café and sit down. They come in right behind me, and one of them takes hold of my beach bag.

I jerk it away and say: Take your hands off! What do you want with my bag? Who are you?

Then he shows me his papers from the Régie des Tabacs. He reaches out for the bag again. What have you got in there?

Nothing.

Let me look.

What for?

The qahouaji comes up and says: Give it to him, Mehdi. Let him look.

So I hand him the bag. He opens it and sees the bread, and the two men just look at each other.

You made it this time, he tells me. Maybe next time you won't.

When that happens, you can shave me without water, I tell him.

We will, he says, and they go out. Then I feel a lot better.

I got up and went back to the oven and gave

the bread to the maallem, and took my kif and tobacco home. There was no more trouble, and I forgot about the Régie des Tabacs.

Aziz and I were trying to get together enough kif so that even when there wasn't any, we could still go on supplying our customers. A month or two later we had about a hundred and twenty-five kilos between us. We'd brought it from up in Beni Guerfat, and it was all at my house.

One afternoon we were sitting in the café, Aziz and I, and several friends. They were playing cards and I was cutting kif, when the men came in.

I had everything spread out in front of me. I was working hard and didn't know they were there.

They looked down at me and began to laugh. I just stared at them.

They picked up everything and wrapped it all in a newspaper. While they were busy doing that, Aziz slipped out and got onto his motor-cycle. There were four men this time, and when they put me into the car they said: Now take us to your house.

When I heard that, my heart stopped. All right, I said.

They drove me home, and two of them went

in with me. My brother was there, and he saw me with my face white, and whispered to me.

Aziz took it all. Don't worry.

I felt a little better.

The two men looked everywhere. Under the beds, in the chests and closets. Finally they went out to the car and told the others they couldn't find anything. Then they had an argument, and all four of them came in this time and began to look again. In each room they left everything in a heap on the floor, and finally they gave up.

Come on, they told me.

I'm not going to leave here until you help me put everything back the way it was, I told them.

They put the things back, and I went with them out to the car, and they took me to the office.

What? cried the Frenchman. You've got him again?

They unwrapped the newspaper and spread out the kif and the tobacco and the board and the knife and the sifter.

You got his tools this time, I see, the Frenchman said. Then he turned to me and began to tell me how young I was to be smoking kif. He told me I'd ruin my health and go crazy and catch all kinds of diseases.

When he finished I said: Kif doesn't drive you crazy. And it doesn't ruin your health. It doesn't hurt you at all if you eat well and sleep enough. What drives you crazy and ruins your health is not having any money.

That's enough! he cried. They never want to hear anybody talk about being poor.

If you don't like my words, I won't talk, I told him. You talk.

You know what we can do to you? We can give you five years in jail.

I told him: You haven't got the right to give me even one day in jail. I smoke kif, and now and then I go and buy a bunch and cut it and smoke it. I don't sell it. One bunch lasts me three or four days. Why don't you go after the men who sell it? You're punishing the ones you ought not to be paying any attention to, and letting the ones who ought to be punished go free.

Like who? said the Frenchman.

Like thieves and murderers and drunks. You don't catch them, but you run after people like me who are just sitting in cafés, not hurting anybody, not making any noise, just minding their own business.

One of the Moslems was looking at me. You like to talk, don't you? he said.

Let him talk, the Frenchman said. Go on, he told me.

If I do, you'll all be against me, I said.

Just go on, he said.

I don't drink alcohol, I told him. Besides, I'm very nervous. I smoke kif to keep calm. Even if somebody comes up and wants a fight, if I've smoked kif I don't pay any attention. I don't know whether I'm sitting down or standing up. If somebody hits me I don't feel it. So there's no way I can do harm to anybody. I just smoke kif and keep quiet. You ought to look for the men who have tons instead of one or two bunches.

The Frenchman wanted to know if I could show him where these people lived who had tons. I said I was sorry, but I didn't know their addresses.

I live off the favors of other people, I told him. When a friend buys a bunch of kif, he buys me one, too. Now and then.

The Frenchman was just looking at me. Weigh the kif, he told his men, and they weighed it. He's got two hundred ten grams here, they said.

Weigh the tobacco.

A hundred twenty grams, they said. Then he turned to me. You know how much that means?

No. How much?

Two hundred ten grams of kif makes four thousand two hundred pesetas, and a hundred twenty grams of tobacco makes six thousand pesetas. That's ten thousand two hundred pesetas. We'll make it an even ten thousand.

I can pay it, I said. But there's one thing.

What's that?

I can pay it if you give me a job and let me pay a little each month. When it's all paid you can fire me.

I see, he said. Yes, yes. You're a very smart young man, aren't you? *Vous êtes très intelligent, monsieur. Très intelligent.*

He was angry, but I went on playing. Anybody who can walk and eat and get around in the world is intelligent, I told him. Even a donkey is intelligent.

Some of the Moslems laughed. *Il se fiche de ma gueule*, the Frenchman was complaining.

It's true! I told them. If a donkey wasn't intelligent, how could he know that *arrah* means go ahead and *cho* means stop? How would he know the difference?

One Moslem said: That's right, and another told him: You're crazy, and they began to have an argument.

The Frenchman was frowning. He yelled at

them, and they were all quiet. Now, he said, talking to me, the last time you made it, but this time you've got to pay.

The last time they just wanted to see what was in the sack inside my beach bag, I told him.

And what was it?

Just pieces of bread. I use them to fish with. Sometimes I eat them myself. Because I have no work. I just sit in the café. And my friends are good to me. Each one helps me a little.

Finally, they took me to a room and shut me in. I sat there for two hours and a half. Then they came and got me and took me back to the Frenchman.

I felt sorry for you, he told me. So you can go.

Do me a favor, I said.

What's that?

Keep the kif and tobacco. Just give me the board and the knife.

Certainly not! What an idea!

But the man who gave them to me is dead. I think more of that board and that knife than I do of anything.

He was frowning at me. And in front of the Moslems standing there he said: That's enough. That's enough. Take everything.

I wrapped it all up. Kif, tobacco, board, sifter and knife. And I thanked him.

Get out of here, he told me.

I went back to the café. Everybody was sitting around looking sad. When they saw me they jumped up. What happened?

I unwrapped the things and showed them to them. It's all here, I said, and I climbed up onto the musicians' platform and asked the qahouaji for a glass of tea. Then I began to cut.

NOTES

THE CANEBRAKE

The husband who keeps his wife in the house and does the marketing himself is a common phenomenon even today. Mrabet's grandfather killed one of his wives for standing fully dressed in the open doorway, looking out into the street.

THE KIF PATCH

This is a commentary by a Riffian on the character of his traditional enemy, the Djibli. The most violent street fights in my quarter of Tangier are the mêlées involving extended families of Riffians and extended families of Djebala. The women and children join in; furniture is hurled from windows and bricks from rooftops.

THE DOCTOR FROM THE CHEMEL

The word *chemel*, while meaning "left" as opposed to "right," is used also to indicate the east. (In Medina, facing Mecca, the east is on the left.) In Morocco, the Rif is referred to as the Chemel.

A Nchaioui is an individual, generally having a strongly psychopathic personality, who has become so thoroughly habituated to cannabis that virtually all his waking hours are passed in the preparation and ingestion of it. He is a stock character in the story-tellers' repertory, probably a contemporary variant of Abu Nowas of *The Thousand and One Nights*, whose taste and capacity for every form of cannabis was boundless. Sometimes he is called the Hacheichi.

HASSAN AND THE AGHREBIA

Aghrebia are small, rather hard cakes, generally given, one to a guest, at a wedding or a naming party for a week-old baby. They come under the category of food, and are not otherwise therapeutic. The household recipe, however does not concur with Si Mokhtar's, which follows:

AGHREBIA

½ kilo kharouah beans
2 kilos whole wheat flour
5 eggs
¼ kilo dried green almonds, previously macerated in mortar
¼ kilo walnuts, chopped
¼ kilo sugar
¼ kilo rancid sheep's butter

Boil Kharouah beans in cauldron of water until the water turns black. This will take more than an hour, and extra water may be needed. Remove beans from water. Put the beans into a skillet and heat them, shaking, until they are completely dried out. Then pound them in a mortar until they are pulverised. Add the flour, sugar and eggs, and stir. To the almonds and walnuts add a handful of unhusked sesame seeds and one grated nutmeg, and pour the mixture into the dough. Now add the black bean-water and mix thoroughly. Spread the rancid sheep's butter over the palms of the hands and rub the palms lightly over the mass of dough. Continue until all the sheep's butter has been rubbed onto the outside of the dough. Sprinkle sugar over the top and cut into strips, which can then be cut into cubes, the cubes being rolled into balls before baking. They need a very hot oven for a half-hour.

THE SEA IN THE STREET

Qoqa, the dried seeds of the red poppy, pulverised. Some smokers lace their kif with the powder, claiming it enhances the effect.

THE DATURA TREES

The slipping of *rhaita* (datura) flowers into the food or drink of one's friends is a standard practical joke.